USBORNE SPOTTER'S STICKER BOOKS
INSECTS

Anthony Wootton

Edited by Rachael Bladon
Designed by Vicki Groombridge

Illustrated by
Phil Weare, Maggie Brand and Sue Testar

Cover design by Adam Constantine
Cover photograph by Claude Nuridsany and Marie Perennou/Science Photo Library
Series editor: Jane Chisholm

How to use this book

There are more than a hundred insect stickers in this book. Using the descriptions and the line drawings, try to match each sticker with the right insect. If you need help, there is a list at the back of the book that tells you which sticker goes with which insect. You can also use this book as a spotter's handbook to make a note of which insects you have seen.

Here are some of the words used to describe parts of an insect.

In this book you will find these signs:

♀ *stands for a female*

♂ *stands for a male*

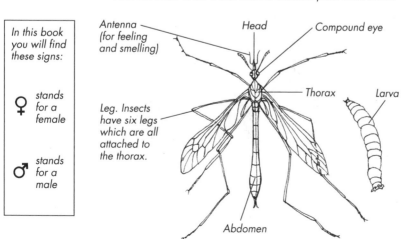

Antenna (for feeling and smelling) *Head* *Compound eye*

Leg. Insects have six legs which are all attached to the thorax.

Thorax *Larva*

Abdomen

Giant cranefly or daddy-long-legs

Many insects have young that look completely different from the adult. These are called larvae. (The name for one is larva.) Other insects have young called nymphs that look like small adults without wings.

BUTTERFLIES

Wall brown ▷

Place	Date

Wingspan: 1¾ in (44-46mm)

This brown butterfly has spots that look like eyes on its front and back wings. It likes dry, open spaces. Related species like the red admiral and the painted lady are found in North America.

◁ Marbled white

Wingspan: 2¹⁄₁₆-2⁵⁄₁₆ in (53-58mm)

The marbled white has marbled black-and-white wings, and belongs to the brush-footed butterfly family. Many similar species occur in North America.

Place	Date

Brown argus ▽

Wingspan: 1⅛in (28-30mm)

This butterfly has brown wings with orange marks near the edges. The males are said to smell of chocolate when they are courting. It is found in Europe and Asia. The American copper is a similar species.

Place	Date

Purple hairstreak ▽

Wingspan: 1⁷⁄₁₆-1⁹⁄₁₆in (36-39mm)

Place	Date

The purple hairstreak flies around the tops of oak trees. It has purplish-blue streaks on its wings.

Alfalfa butterfly ▷

Wingspan: 1⅝-2⅜ in (40-60mm)

The alfalfa butterfly has pale orange wings with dark edges. The larva feeds on alfalfa, white clover and related plants.

Place	Date

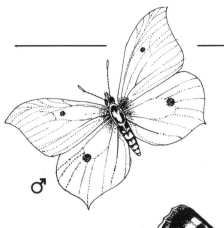

◁ Brimstone
Wingspan: 2$\frac{5}{16}$-2$\frac{7}{16}$in (58-62mm)

This large yellow butterfly is rare in North America, occasionally straying into Florida and Texas. The female is pale greeny-white.

◁ Peacock
Wingspan: 2$\frac{7}{16}$-2$\frac{11}{16}$in (62-68mm)

The adult peacock hibernates in the winter. Its large wings are red with brightly colored eye-like markings. The buckeye of North America is a similar species.

Silver-bordered fritillary ▷
Wingspan: 1$\frac{5}{8}$-1$\frac{3}{4}$in (42-46mm)

This butterfly has black markings on top of its orange-brown wings, and silver spots underneath. The adults are found in bogs, marshy areas, and forest meadows.

▽ Cabbage butterfly
Wingspan: 1$\frac{7}{8}$-2in (48-50mm)

You might see this common white butterfly flitting around gardens, especially near cabbages. Its front wings have black tips.

Comma　　　　　△
Wingspan: 1$\frac{7}{8}$-2$\frac{1}{16}$in (47-52mm)

This ragged-winged butterfly has a silver comma on the underside of its hind wings.

MOTHS

Hummingbird hawk-moth

Wingspan: 1¾in (45mm) ▽

You might see this little moth hovering over flowers and beating its wings like a hummingbird. It has brown front wings and orange back wings.

Place	Date

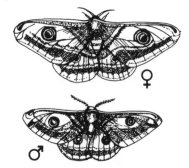

◁ **Emperor moth**

Wingspan: female 2¾in (70mm)
male 2³⁄₁₆in (55mm)

The male emperor moth has orange back wings, spots that look like eyes on each wing, and antennae that are like feathers. The female is bigger, with eye-like spots and a blue head. The polyphemus moth is a related species.

Place	Date

Lobster moth ▷

Wingspan: 2⁹⁄₁₆-2¾in (65-70mm)

The lobster moth is a dull gray-brown color. It takes its name from the larva's tail end, which looks like a lobster's claw. Many similar species occur in North America.

Place	Date

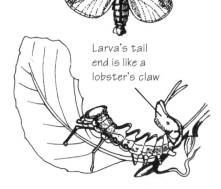

Larva's tail end is like a lobster's claw

Peach blossom ▽

Wingspan: 1⅜in (35mm)

The peach blossom can be found in woodland. It takes its name from the pink spots on its brown front wings. It is found in Europe and across Asia to Japan.

Place	Date

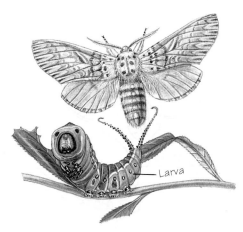

Larva

Puss moth

◁

Wingspan: 2⁹⁄₁₆-3⅛in (65-80mm)

The puss moth is pale pink and gray, and is common throughout Britain. When its larva is alarmed, thin red "whips" stick out of its tails.

Place	Date

Clifden nonpareil
or blue underwing ▷

Place	Date

Wingspan: 3⁹/₁₆in (90mm)

This moth is rare, and is found in eastern or southern England. It has mottled gray front wings and dark back wings with pale blue stripes around them. The white underwing is a similar species in North America.

Red underwing ▽

Wingspan: 3¹/₈in (80mm)

This moth flashes its red-and-black back wings when it is threatened by birds. The color of its front wings matches the bark of trees.

Place	Date

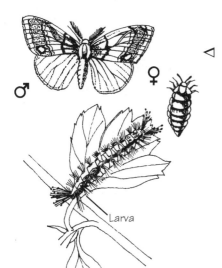

♂   ♀

Larva

◁ Vapourer

Wingspan: 1³/₈in (35mm)

The male vapourer has brown wings, but the female only has wing stubs and cannot fly.

Place	Date

Oak eggar ▽

Wingspan: 2-2⁹/₁₆in (50-65mm)

The oak eggar has brown wings, with yellow edges and a white spot on each front wing. The male's antennae are like feathers.

Place	Date

Alfalfa looper △

Wingspan: 1⁹/₁₆in (40mm)

The alfalfa looper is a dull-colored moth, with white markings on its front wings. It flies by day and can often be seen in late summer taking nectar from flowers.

Place	Date

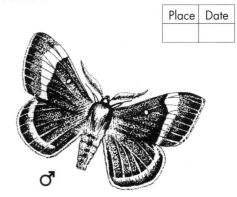

♂

MOTHS

Lappet ▷

Place	Date

Wingspan: 2³⁄₈-2³⁄₄in (60-70mm)

The lappet holds its veined brown wings so that they overlap, making it look like a bunch of leaves. Its larva has a long green part called a "lappet" sticking out of its head.

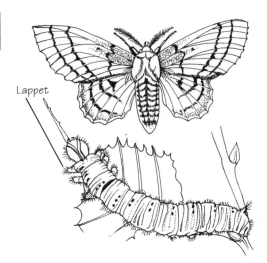

Lappet

△

Wood tiger

Wingspan: 1³⁄₈-1⁹⁄₁₆ (35-40mm)

This brown-and-cream patterned moth is common in open woodland and on hillsides.

Place	Date

Woolly bear

◁ Garden tiger

Wingspan: 2³⁄₈-2³⁄₄in (60-70mm)

The garden tiger has orange back wings with black spots on them. Its front wings are mottled brown and cream. This moth's larva is called "woolly bear".

Place	Date

♂

Swallow-tailed moth ▽

Wingspan: 2³⁄₁₆in (56mm)

This pale-colored moth has large petal-shaped wings which make it look like a butterfly. It flies in a weak, fluttering way.

Place	Date

Ghost moth △

Wingspan: 2-2³⁄₈in (50-60mm)

Place	Date

The female ghost moth's wings are browner than the white male's, and it is therefore better camouflaged. This moth is not often seen, even though it is extremely common.

Cinnabar ▷

Wingspan: 1⁹⁄₁₆-1¾in (40-45mm)

You might see this moth flying short distances by day. Its yellow and black larva can be seen on ragwort. Related species are found worldwide.

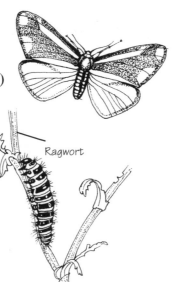

Ragwort

Place	Date

Six-spot burnet ▽

Wingspan: 1⅜in (35mm)

The six-spot burnet takes its name from the six red spots it has on each brown front wing. Its back wings are red, and its bright color warns birds that it tastes bad. The grape leaf skeletenizer is a similar species in North America.

Place	Date

Markings like a human skull

◁ Death's head hawk-moth

Place	Date

Wingspan: 4-4⅞in (100-125mm)

This rare moth is named after the markings on its thorax, which look like a human skull. Its front wings are patterned brown, and its back wings are light brown with darker stripes. The death's head hawk-moth lays its eggs on potato leaves. It is related to the hornworm moth of North America

Forester ▷

Wingspan: 1-1¹⁄₁₆in (25-27mm)

This little moth has green front wings and pale back wings. It can often be seen flying over meadows in the summer in Europe and Asia.

Place	Date

▽ Eyed hawk-moth

Wingspan: 3-3⅛in (75-80mm)

The eyed hawk-moth has large eye-like markings on its pink and brown back wings. It flashes these to frighten off its enemies.

Place	Date

BEETLES

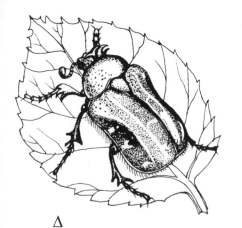

Longhorn beetle ▷

Length: ¼-3in (6-75mm)

The longhorn beetle comes in many colors and sizes.

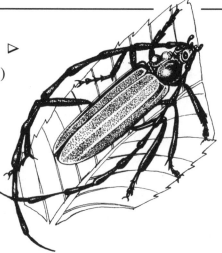

Place	Date

Δ

Rose chafer

Length: ⁹/₁₆-¹³/₁₆in (14-20mm)

The rose chafer's wing cases look almost square in shape, but the front of its thorax is very round. It is related to the June beetle of North America.

Place	Date

Δ

Ladybird beetle

Length: ¼in (6-7mm)

The red ladybird, with its black spots, is very common in North America. It can be seen on sunny days.

Place	Date

Japanese beetle ▽

Length: ¹¹/₁₆-1⅛in (18-29mm)

You might see this beetle flying up to lit windows in the early summer. It has brown wing cases and a black head with fur underneath its thorax.

Place	Date

Place	Date

Δ

Stag beetle

Length: 1-2¹⁵/₁₆in (25-75mm)

Place	Date

Male stag beetles defend themselves fiercely if they are attacked, but sometimes have difficulty in righting themselves if overturned.

▽ ## Water beetle

Length: ¼in (7-8mm)

Water beetles are very common, and vary in color from brown to black. This one has a brown body with black markings on its wing.

Great diving beetle ▷

Length: 1³/₁₆-1³/₈in (30-35mm)

Larva

You might find the great diving beetle in lakes and ponds. Its body is black with light brown edges, and it has brown legs and antennae.

Place	Date

Place	Date

Cardinal beetle

Length: ⁵/₈in (15-17mm) △

There are different kinds of cardinal beetles. This one has a long red body, and antennae with branches all along them. It can be found on flowers and under bark.

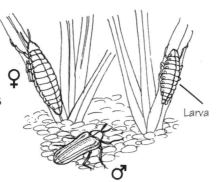
♀
Larva
♂

◁ Glowworm

Male length: ⁵/₈in (15mm)
Female length: ³/₄in (20mm)

The female glowworm has a long brown body with no wings or wing-cases. She attracts the male with her glowing tail.

Place	Date

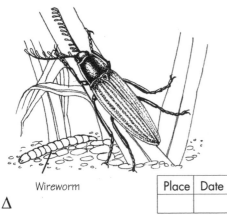
Wireworm

△

Click beetle or skip-jack

Length: ⁹/₁₆-¹¹/₁₆in (14-18mm)

This click beetle has a sleek green body, with small branches all along its antennae. Its larva is called "wireworm".

Place	Date

Red and black burying beetle ▷

Length: ⁹/₁₆-¹³/₁₆in (15-20mm)

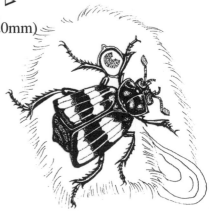

This beetle has two large red streaks across its black wing cases. It feeds on dead animals, biting their flesh and then burying their bodies.

Place	Date

◁ Douglas fir borer

Place	Date

Length: ⅝in (15mm)

This beetle looks like a wasp, with yellow stripes along its brown body. The larvae bore into Douglas fir, where they feed on the wood.

Place	Date

Δ

Bloody-nosed beetle

Length: ⅜-½in (10-20mm)

When this beetle is threatened, it shoots a bright red fluid from its mouth. The bloody-nosed beetle has round black wing cases and a rectangular black section behind its head.

Place	Date

Colorado potato beetle

Length: ⅜-½in (10-12mm) ▷

You can recognize a colorado potato beetle by its rounded body and the dark and light brown stripes along its wing cases.

Larva

Green tortoise beetle ▽

Place	Date

Length: ¼-⁵⁄₁₆in (6-8mm)

This green beetle has a rounded body and, when its legs and antennae are hidden, it looks like a tortoise. Its larva has a fork in its tail for holding skins and droppings.

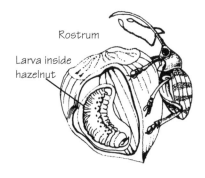

Rostrum

Larva inside hazelnut

Nut weevil Δ

Place	Date

Length: ⅜in (10mm)

The female nut weevil has a very long snout and a rounded brown body. She uses her snout (called a "rostrum") to make holes in young hazelnuts, where she lays her single egg. The larva then grows inside the nut, eating the kernel.

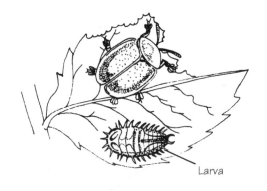

Larva

Devil's coach horse or cocktail beetle ▷

Length: 1-1³⁄₁₆in (25-30mm)

Place	Date

This black beetle can often be found in yards. It has a long abdomen, which can release a poisonous liquid.

Larva

◁ Horned dung beetle or minotaur beetle

Length: ½-¹¹⁄₁₆in (12-18mm)

Place	Date

This black beetle has broad ribbed wing cases, thick horny legs and large horns around its head.

Giant water scavenger beetle

Length: 1⁵⁄₁₆-1½in (34-38mm) ▽

Place	Date

This beetle has a large black body, with hairy back legs and claws on its front legs. It feeds on small animals that live in the water, or on their remains.

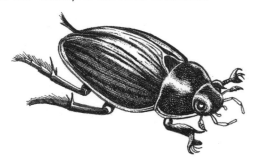

Death watch beetle △

Length: ¼-³⁄₈in (7-10mm)

Place	Date

The noise this beetle makes, knocking its head on the walls of the tunnels it builds, was once thought to mean that someone was about to die. The death watch beetle is mottled dark and light brown. It eats the wood in barns and old, damp, timber buildings.

Rove beetle ▷

Length: ¹³⁄₁₆in (20mm)

Place	Date

There are different kinds of rove beetles. This one has red eyes and legs, a red section in the thorax and a long black tail. Rove beetles eat dead animals and birds.

BUGS

Backswimmer ▷

Place	Date

Length: ⁹⁄₁₆in (15mm)

The backswimmer's body is kind of like a little boat. It swims on its back, with the tips of its legs clinging to the underside of the water surface. Its back legs are shaped like paddles and fringed with hairs. The backswimmer can be found in pools, canals, ditches and water tanks, but if its home dries up, it can fly away.

Creeping water bug ▽

Length: ½-⅝in (12-16mm)

The creeping water bug is common in ponds, where it feeds on small animals that live in the water. It has short legs, and the front ones are rounded and very sharp. The creeping water bug can stab you with its jaws.

Place	Date

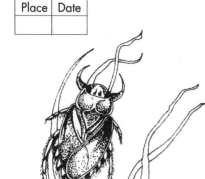

◁ Water strider

Place	Date

Length: ⁵⁄₁₆-⅜in (8-10mm)

Water striders are small, with very long legs and thin bodies. Their front legs are specially shaped to catch dead or dying insects that fall on the water surface.

Water cricket ▷

Length: ¼in (6-7mm)

The water cricket has long legs, and a dark body with two light brown stripes along it. You can find it on the surface of still water, eating insects and spiders.

Place	Date

Black and red froghopper ▷

Length: ⅜in (9-10mm)

This red-and-black striped bug jumps when it is disturbed. Most froghopper nymphs produce froth.

Place	Date

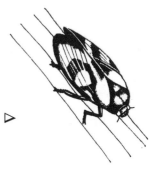

1

Larva

2

3

4

5

Pot

6

Larva

7

8

9

10

11

12

13

14

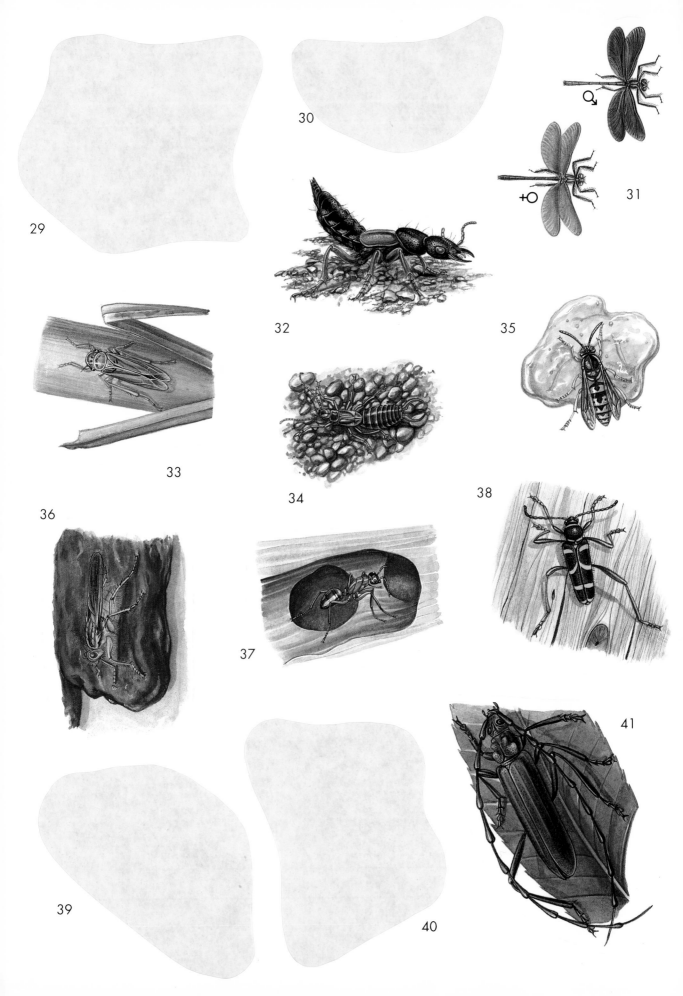

29

30

31

32

33

34

35

36

37

38

39

40

41

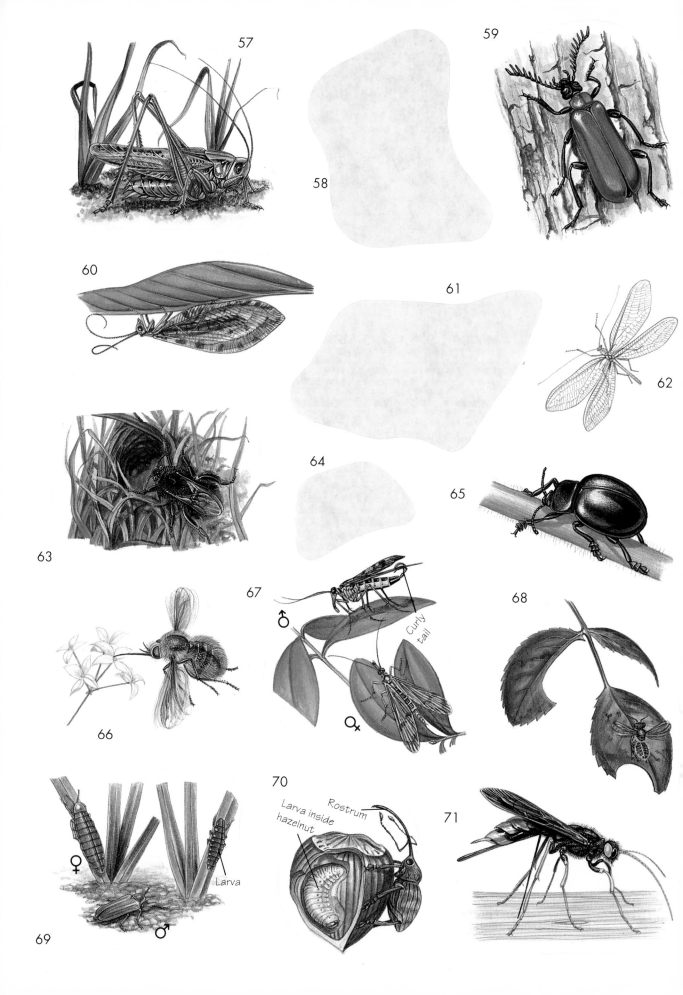

57

58

59

60

61

62

63

64

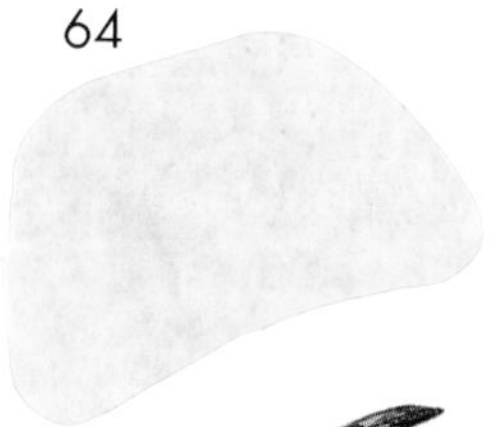

65

66

67

♂

♀

Curly tail

68

69

♀

♂

Larva

70

Larva inside hazelnut

Rostrum

71

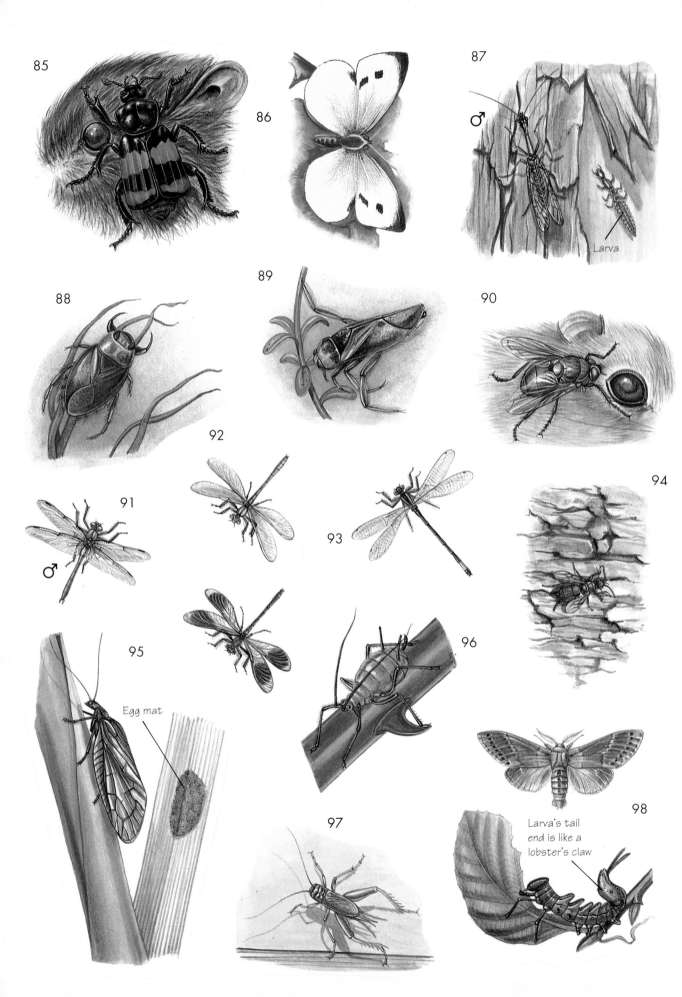

85

86

87 ♂ Larva

88

89

90

91 ♂

92

93

94

95 Egg mat

96

97

98 Larva's tail end is like a lobster's claw

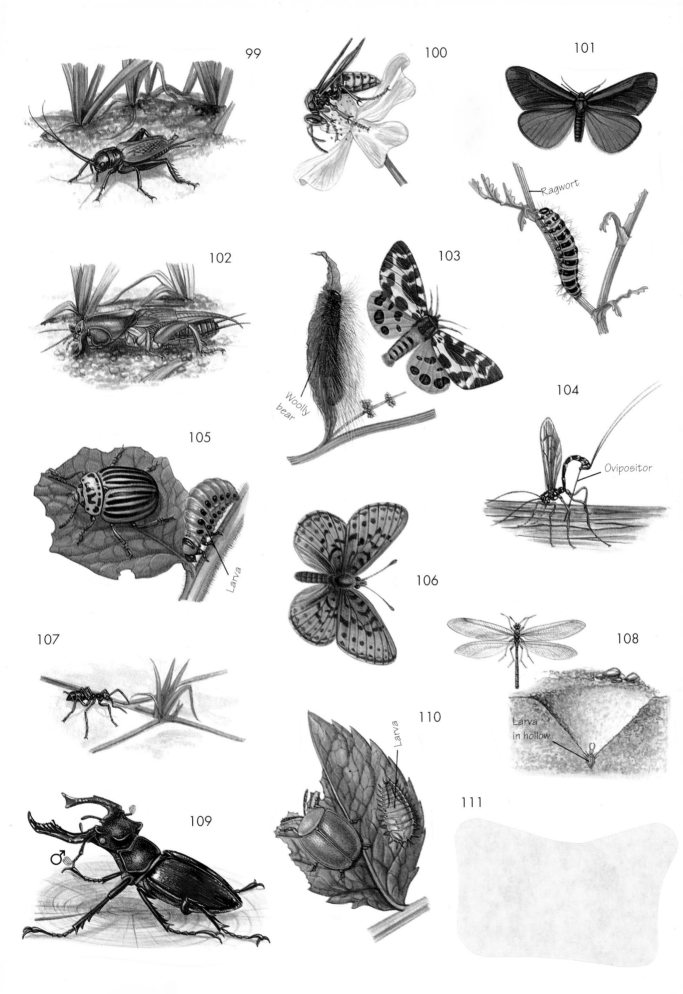

99

100

101

Ragwort

102

103

Woolly
bear

104

Ovipositor

105

Larva

106

107

110

Larva

108

Larva
in hollow

109

111

Lappet

72

73

74

♀

♂

75

76

77

78

80

♂

♀

81

79

82

83

84

42

43

44

45

46

47

48

49

50

51

52

53

54 ♀

55

Breathing
tube

56

15

16

17
♀
♂
Larva

18

19
♂

20
Marble
gall

21
♂

22

23

24

25
Leatherjacket

26
Wireworm

27

28

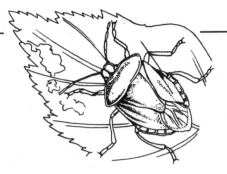

Green stinkbug

Place	Date	▷

Length: ¹/₂-¹¹/₁₆in (13-18mm)

You might find the green stinkbug in crop fields, orchards and gardens. It can give out a foul smell when disturbed.

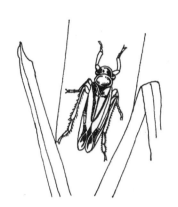

Black bean aphid or blackfly ▽

Length: ¹/₁₆-¹/₈in (2-3mm)

You might find colonies of this tiny bug on broad beans or thistles. The black bean aphid has a rounded black body.

Place	Date

Length: ¹/₄-³/₈in (6-9mm)

This bug has a long straight green body with brown legs. It is common, and feeds on grasses and rushes.

Place	Date

Rose aphid or greenfly ▷

Length: ¹/₁₆-¹/₈in (2-3mm)

The rose aphid, or greenfly, is shaped like a bulb, and can be green or pinkish. Its antennae are long compared to its body. This bug feeds on roses in the spring, making itself a pest. It produces honeydew, which ants eat.

Place	Date

Breathing tube

Water scorpion ▷

Length: ¹¹/₁₆-⁷/₈in (18-22mm)

The water scorpion has claw-like front legs which it uses to catch small fishes, tadpoles and insect larvae. It has a brown body with a long breathing tube sticking out behind.

Place	Date

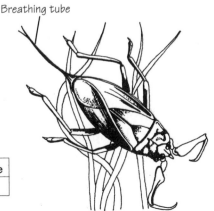

13

DRAGONFLIES, DAMSELFLIES

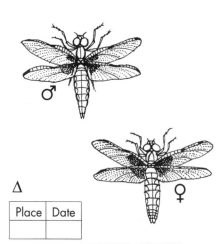

Place	Date

Broad-bodied libellula

Wingspan: 3in (75mm)

The broad-bodied libellula is similar to the widow of North America. The male has a broad, pale blue body with yellow markings on it, and the female is yellow.

Half-banded toper ▷

Wingspan: 2³⁄₁₆in (55mm)

You can find the half-banded toper around weedy ponds or ditches in marshy areas, but it is getting rarer. It has a golden-brown colored body and transparent wings.

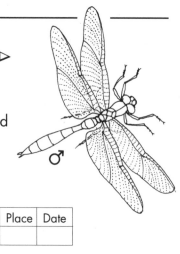

Place	Date

◁ Green Darner

Wingspan: 4⁵⁄₁₆in (110mm)

This dragonfly has a bright green thorax and abdomen of blue to purplish-gray.

Place	Date

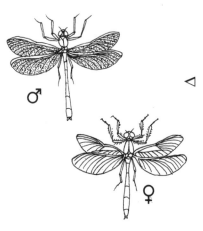

Place	Date

◁ Black-wing damselfly

Wingspan: 2¹⁄₄-2¹⁄₂in (58-63mm)

The black-wing damselfly has a green body and wings with long thick veins, which are brown on the female.

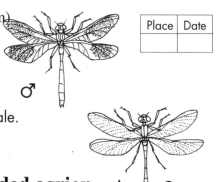

Place	Date

Banded agrion △

Wingspan: 2³⁄₈-2⁵⁄₈in (60-65mm)

The male has a blue body and bright blue flashes on each of its wings, while the female is green with transparent green wings. The banded agrion is related to the ruby spot of North America.

Common forktail

Wingspan: 1³⁄₈in (35mm) ▷

This damselfly has transparent wings, and a blue tip on its long body. It can be found resting on plants in wet areas.

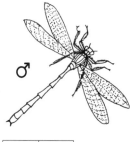

Place	Date

Bees, Wasps

Red-tailed bumblebee ▷

Length: 7/8in (22mm)

Place	Date

This bee has a big, black, furry body with an orange-red tip. It is common in yards. The queen makes her nest in a hole in the ground.

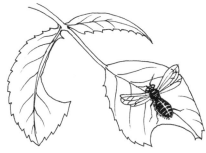

Potter wasp ▷

Male length: 1/2in (12mm)
Female length: 9/16in (14mm)

Place	Date

The potter wasp makes small clay pots for its larvae. It then fills the pots with little caterpillars which it paralyzes with its sting. This potter wasp has black and yellow stripes on the tip of its abdomen.

Ruby-tailed wasp ▷

Length: 1/2in (12mm)

Place	Date

This wasp takes its name from its bright red abdomen, but it is also known as a "cuckoo-wasp". This is because the female lays her egg in the nest of another bee or wasp. The larva then eats the food, egg or larva of that bee or wasp.

◁ Leaf-cutter bee

Male length: 3/8in (10mm)
Female length: 7/16in (11mm)

Place	Date

The leaf-cutter bee cuts semi-circular pieces from rose leaves to make cylinders where the female lays a single egg. It stores these cylinders in hollow stems and dead wood. This leaf-cutter bee is small and green.

Pot

◁ Thread-waisted wasp

Length: 1 1/8-1 3/16in (28-30mm)

Place	Date

The thread-waisted wasp digs in the sand and lays a single egg on top of a paralyzed caterpillar, which the larva then eats. This sand wasp has a pointed snout and a bulb-shaped tip on its abdomen.

WASPS

Oak marble gall-wasp ▽

Length: ³/₁₆in (4mm)

This gall-wasp has a small reddish-brown body and gray wings. It lays its egg in a leaf bud, and as the larva feeds, the tree forms a solid lump around it.

Place	Date

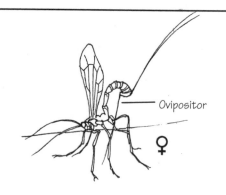
Ovipositor
♀

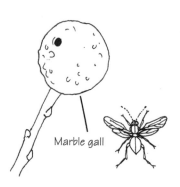
Marble gall

Ichneumon wasp △

Place	Date

Length: ⅞-1³/₁₆in (22-30mm)

This large, long-legged wasp has an extension, called an "ovipositor", which is longer than its body. It uses this to pierce holes in pine trees and to lay its eggs inside the tree.

◁ Hornet

Length: ⅞-1³/₁₆in (22-30mm)

The hornet is very large and has brown and yellow markings on its abdomen. It is less likely to sting than the common wasp.

Place	Date

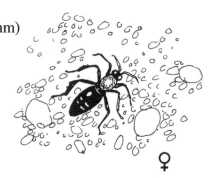
♀

German yellowjacket

Length: ⁹/₁₆-¹³/₁₆in (15-20mm) ▷

This wasp has yellow and black markings along its abdomen. It is commonly an uninvited guest at picnics.

Place	Date

Velvet ant △

Place	Date

Length: ⁹/₁₆in (15mm)

Although its female has no wings, the velvet ant is actually a wasp. The female has a red rounded thorax, and a black abdomen marked with four light flecks and a light ring. The velvet ant can give you a nasty sting.

WASPS, SAWFLY, ANTS

Blue horntail

Place	Date

▷

Length: $^{13}/_{16}$-1in (20-25mm)

The head, thorax and first two segments of the male's abdomen are deep metallic blue. The female is blue all over. The blue horntail can be found in pine forests.

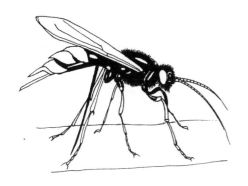

◁ ## Giant wood wasp or horntail

Place	Date

Length: 1-1$^1/_4$in (25-32mm)

The giant wood wasp, or horntail, is large, black and hairy, with yellow stripes on its abdomen and a yellow pad behind its eye. Its larvae feed on wood for up to three years.

Birch sawfly

Place	Date

▷

Length: $^{13}/_{16}$-$^7/_8$in (20-23mm)

The birch sawfly has a dark body with a small yellow fleck around the top of its abdomen. Its larva has six pairs of extra "prolegs", as well as three pairs of true legs. It feeds on birch leaves in late summer.

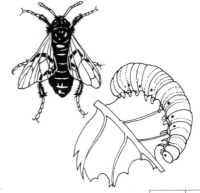

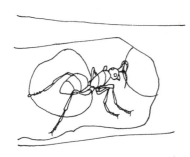

◁ ## Carpenter ant

Place	Date

Length: $^5/_{16}$-$^{11}/_{16}$in (8-18mm)

The carpenter ant's thorax is reddish-brown, while its head and lower body are much darker. It nests in pine tree trunks, hollowing them out and often making the whole tree fall down.

Black ant

Place	Date

▷

Length: $^1/_8$-$^3/_8$in (3-9mm)

This ant is black, and common in yards. The males die after mating, and the queens then start new nests or colonies on their own.

TRUE FLIES

◁ Gray flesh fly

Length: ¼-¹¹/₁₆in (6-17mm)

Place	Date

The gray flesh fly has gray and black markings on its body, and reddish-brown eyes. It is common, and lays its eggs in carrion (dead rotting meat).

Hover fly ▷

Length: ³/₈-⁹/₁₆in (10-14mm)

Place	Date

This hover fly is brown, with three light stripes on each side of its abdomen. Hover flies can hover in the air as if they were not moving.

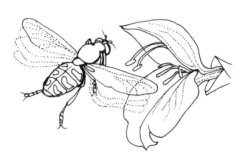

Greenbottle fly ▽

Length: ¼-⁷/₁₆in (11mm

Place	Date

This fly is bottle green and can be found among flowers. Most species of greenbottle fly lay their eggs in carrion (dead rotting meat).

Place	Date

Horse fly ▵

Length: ¹³/₁₆-1in (20-25mm)

A loud hum warns you that the female horse fly is about to bite you. The horse fly has a dark brown body, with light brown edges on each segment of its abdomen, and large green eyes.

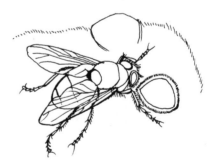

◁ Dung fly

Length: ³/₈-¹/₂in (10-12mm)

You can find the dung fly around fresh cowpatties, where the female lays her eggs. This one has a bright golden-colored body. When dung flies are disturbed, they rise in a buzzing mass, but soon settle again.

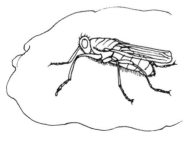

Place	Date

18

TRUE FLIES, ANT-LION

Bee fly ▷

Length: ³/₈-⁷/₁₆in (10-11mm)

Place	Date

The bee fly has a round furry body, and flies around garden flowers looking for nectar in early spring.

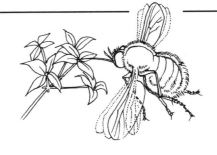

◁ Giant cranefly or daddy-long-legs

Length: 1¼-1⁹/₁₆in (30-40mm)

This large fly has a long spindly body and very long legs. It is often found near water. Its larvae are called "leatherjackets", and they eat root crops and grass roots.

Place	Date

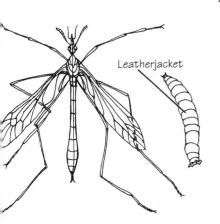

Leatherjacket

Common gnat △ or mosquito

Length: ¼in (6-7mm)

Place	Date

This common gnat is small, with a golden-brown body and very long thin legs. The female sucks blood from people and animals.

Black and yellow cranefly ▷

Length: ¹¹/₁₆-¹³/₁₆in (18-20mm)

This cranefly has a long body, with black and yellow markings, and very long thin legs. In the summer, it can often be seen joined end-to-end with another cranefly while mating.

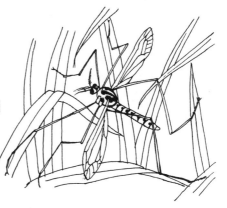

Place	Date

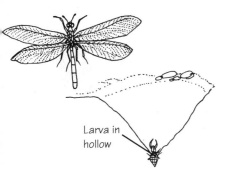

Larva in hollow

◁ Ant-lion

Length: 1³/₈in (35mm)

Place	Date

The ant-lion is long, with four broad white wings. Its larva traps ants and other insects in a sandy hollow and then sucks them dry.

SCORPION FLY, LACY-WINGED INSECTS

Lacewings, snake flies and alder flies all have wings with fine, delicately patterned veins.

Scorpion fly ▽

Length: ¹¹/₁₆-⁷/₈in (18-22mm)

Place	Date

The scorpion fly is so-called because of the male's tail, which curls up like a scorpion's. The male has a long yellow body with black markings, and a long " beak".

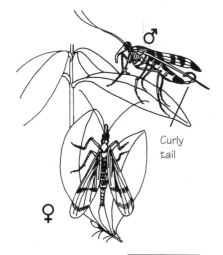

Curly tail

♂

♀

Giant lacewing ▽

Length: ⁹/₁₆in (15mm)

Place	Date

You are most likely to spot the giant lacewing by night. It has large see-through wings covered in brown lace-like veins, and very long, wavy antennae.

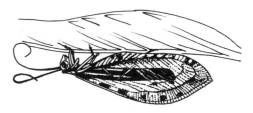

Place	Date

▽ ## Green lacewing

Length: ⁹/₁₆in (15mm)

The green lacewing has four wings covered with green lace-like veins. You can find it mainly around gardens and hedges. Green lacewings often come into houses to hibernate through the winter.

Snake fly ▽

Place	Date

Length: ⁹/₁₆-¹³/₁₆in (15-20mm)

The snake fly is so-called because when it bends its head and thorax, it looks like a cobra. This one has a long head and thorax and thin transparent wings.

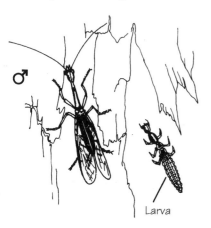

♂

Larva

Alder fly ▷

Length: ¹³/₁₆in (20mm)

The alder fly lays its eggs in mats on the stems of water plants. It flies in a slow, heavy way. This alder fly has large brownish wings and long antennae.

Place	Date

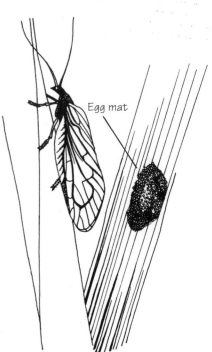

Egg mat

MAYFLY, STONEFLY, CRICKETS

Mayfly ▷

Length: 1 9/16 (40mm)

Place	Date

The adult mayfly does not live for long - sometimes for as little as a few hours. Its nymphs live in ponds and streams. This mayfly is large, with long tails and transparent brown striped wings.

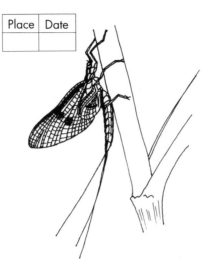

Stonefly

Place	Date

▽

Length: 7/8in (22 mm)

The stonefly has long overlapping wings. Its nymphs have long tails and live on the river bottom, feeding on other small animals.

House cricket

◁ Length: 5/8in (16mm)

Place	Date

You might hear the shrill song of the house cricket in and around greenhouses, heated buildings and garbage heaps. It has a light brown body with dark markings, broad spiny back legs and short tails.

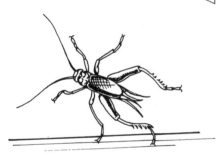

Field cricket ▷

Length: 3/4in (20mm)

Place	Date

The field cricket has a black body and legs, long antennae and brown wing cases. The male "sings" to attract a female by rubbing its wing cases together.

◁ ## Mole cricket

Place	Date

Length: 1 1/2-1 5/8in (38-42mm)

The outside of the mole cricket's thorax has grown forward, over its head, looking like an armor case. This cricket has front feet shaped like spades, which it uses for digging. The male has a long whirring call.

21

BUSH CRICKETS, GRASSHOPPER, STICK INSECT

Place	Date

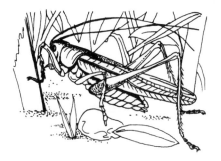

◁ **Fork-tailed bush katydid**
Length: 1¾-1⅞in (45-47mm)

The Fork-tailed bush katydid has long wings and antennae, and long thin back legs. It makes a loud, shrill noise, moves slowly and never flies very far.

Wart-biter
Length: 1⁵⁄₁₆-1⅜in (34-35mm)

Place	Date

▷

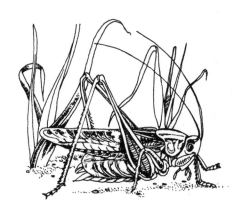

The wart-biter looks very like the fork-tailed bush katydid, but it is smaller, with shorter antennae and dark markings on its green wings. It may bite when it is handled. People in Sweden used to use this insect to bite their warts.

◁ **Alutacea bird grasshopper**
Length: 1¼-1¾in (30-45mm)

This grasshopper's favorite food is grasses. It can fly rapidly over great distances, which is how it gets its name.

Place	Date

Stick insect ▷
Length: up to 5⅞in (150mm)

The stick insect is so-called because its very long, thin, green body looks like a stick with thin legs attached. Oak leaves are the favorite food of most stick insects.

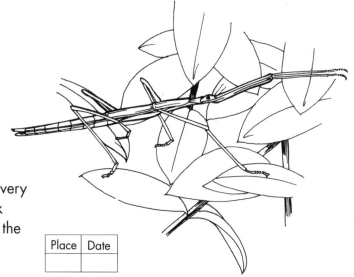

Place	Date

PRAYING MANTIS, COCKROACHES, EARWIG

Praying mantis ▷

Place	Date

Length: 2³⁄₈-3¹⁄₈in (60-80mm)

The praying mantis has a long green body, with a small head and large front legs. It holds these together as if it is praying while it waits for its insect prey to come near.

◁ Oriental cockroach

Place	Date

Length: 1in (25mm)

The oriental cockroach is large, black and rounded, with spiny legs and long antennae. Its head is covered by the outside of the thorax, which has grown forward, looking like a helmet. It eats waste in houses and other buildings. It does not fly.

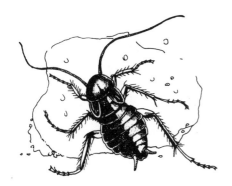

German cockroach ▽

Length: ¹⁄₂in (13mm)

The German cockroach has a light brown body, with two dark streaks on its head, and long folded wing cases. In spite of its name, it probably comes from North Africa or the Middle East.

Place	Date

◁ American cockroach

Length: 1¹⁄₂-2in (38-50mm)

The American cockroach is a strong flyer. It is generally found in heavily populated areas.

Place	Date

Common earwig ▷

Length: ⁹⁄₁₆in (15mm)

The common earwig is brown and has tiny wing cases and a long abdomen with pincers at the end. It spreads these and lifts them above its body when it feels threatened. The common earwig scavenges on small insects, fruits and leaves.

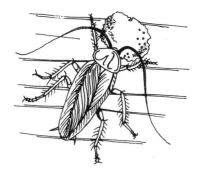

Place	Date

CHECKLIST

1 Devil's coach horse or cocktail beetle
2 Purple hairstreak
3 Fork-tailed bush katydid
4 Birch sawfly
5 Potter wasp
6 Great diving beetle
7 Thread-waisted wasp
8 Eyed hawk-moth
9 Green stinkbug
10 Horned dung beetle or minotaur beetle
11 Forester
12 Oriental cockroach
13 Alfalfa looper
14 Praying mantis
15 Black bean aphid or blackfly
16 Marbled white
17 Vapourer
18 Blue horntail
19 Brimstone
20 Oak marble gall-wasp
21 Oak eggar
22 Wall brown
23 Common gnat or mosquito
24 Peach blossom
25 Giant cranefly or daddy-long-legs
26 Click beetle or skip-jack
27 Stonefly
28 Grey flesh fly
29 Puss moth
30 Ghost moth
31 Black-wing damselfly
32 Rove beetle
33 Green leafhopper
34 Common earwig
35 German yellowjacket
36 Dung fly

37 Carpenter ant
38 Douglas fir borer
39 Ladybird beetle
40 Comma
41 Longhorn beetle
42 German cockroach
43 Hummingbird hawk-moth
44 Giant water scavenger beetle
45 Water cricket
46 Water beetle
47 Half-banded toper
48 Rose chafer
49 Death watch beetle
50 Six-spot burnet
51 Black and red froghopper
52 Clifden nonpareil or blue underwing
53 Peacock
54 Velvet ant
55 Wood tiger
56 Water scorpion
57 Wart-biter
58 Alfalfa butterfly
59 Cardinal beetle
60 Giant lacewing
61 Death's head hawk-moth
62 Green lacewing
63 Red-tailed bumblebee
64 Brown argus
65 Bloody-nosed beetle
66 Bee fly
67 Scorpion fly
68 Leaf-cutter bee
69 Glow-worm
70 Nut weevil
71 Giant wood wasp or horntail
72 Lappet
73 Mayfly

74 Emperor moth
75 Japanese beetle
76 Water strider
77 Stick insect
78 American cockroach
79 Alutacea bird grasshopper
80 Broad-bodied libellula
81 Hover fly
82 Red underwing
83 Horse fly
84 Black and yellow cranefly
85 Red and black burying beetle
86 Cabbage butterfly
87 Snake fly
88 Creeping water bug
89 Backswimmer
90 Greenbottle fly
91 Green darner
92 Banded agrion
93 Common forktail
94 Ruby-tailed wasp
95 Alder fly
96 Rose aphid or greenfly
97 House cricket
98 Lobster moth
99 Field cricket
100 Hornet
101 Cinnabar
102 Mole cricket
103 Garden tiger
104 Ichneumon wasp
105 Colorado potato beetle
106 Silver-bordered fritillary
107 Black ant
108 Ant-lion
109 Stag beetle
110 Green tortoise beetle
111 Swallow-tailed moth

First published in 1994 by Usborne Publishing Ltd., 83-85 Saffron Hill, London EC1N 8RT, England.
Copyright © 1994, 1986, 1979 Usborne Publishing Ltd.

Printed in Italy.